Sacred Memoirs of
a Retired Failure

Sacred Memoirs of a Retired Failure

Published by The Conrad Press in the United Kingdom 2020

Tel: +44(0)1227 472 874
www.theconradpress.com
info@theconradpress.com

ISBN 978-1-915494-14-6

Typesetting and Cover Design by:
Charlotte Mouncey, www.bookstyle.co.uk

The Conrad Press logo was designed by Maria Priestley.

Printed and bound in Great Britain by Clays Ltd, Elcograf S.p.A.

Dedicated to those who find retirement exciting,
courageously facing challenges whilst
seeking new horizons.

Sacred Memoirs of a Retired Failure

A.N. Drew

Chapter One

Father Dougal stared out of his cottage window, on a frosty January morning in Wiltshire. As a low Anglican he hated being called Father, and he certainly bore no resemblance to Father Dougal of *Father Ted* fame. His mother loved *The Magic Roundabout* so re-named him Dougal instead of the baptized Douglas but he preferred Doug as in Rev Doug.

Mothers seem to instinctively know if their children are to be ordained or whatever, they sense it. They do not know when or where but they know. Most do.

Retirement had just arrived. His wife Mary had passed away the previous year of inoperable brain cancer which really tested his faith. His daughters Angela and Beth had their own families to cope with. He visited them from time to time, and in the summer hoped they would come to see him with his three grandchildren who could play in the tiny garden. They cared about each other but did not live in each other's pockets.

Angela, the eldest, had rung Beth on her mobile a couple of weeks ago asking, 'What are we going to do about Dad?' to which there was no coherent reply, or decision. Dad would do his own thing.

Three weeks and counting. So this is retirement, when you wonder how you had the time to manage work as well as everything else. Mary's estate had enabled him to buy the small cottage in the countryside near Amesbury and he had moved in and settled. Well some boxes still lying around but on the whole shipshape. Mary would have had it all sorted by now, boxes at the local tip, everything stored away, the place clean and tidy.

They had moved several times in their thirty-six years of marriage but this was the first place he could call his. As far away from previous work environments as possible.

Mary's parents had known they would need funds for a place to retire, though Doug had a mixture of gratitude and regret that she never saw it. His faith had been battered but was strong enough to ride the storm. He read recently that without the inner discipline of faith, most lives end in negativity, blaming, or deep cynicism - without even knowing it. Wherever you are now Mary, you will be smiling. That kept him going.

Strange times, almost surreal. Loneliness and longing, hope and despair. The thoughts of despair could be overwhelming, dark foreboding which made the present almost unbearable. Making sense of the present whilst daring to hope there can be some kind of future. Trying to answer questions such as faith and hope. He knew the answer, or thought he did.

You cannot have hope without faith. Faith is shaped by experience, whereas hope is the product of desiring a future state of affairs. But in spite of the importance of faith and hope, love is even more crucial. They had loved and been in love. For almost forty years. Shared a common faith, always had hope.

Sometimes he felt Mary's faith was even stronger than his; she never doubted, never questioned his calling, never complained though some people could be so cruel. She always made sense of the nonsensical. She would make sense of his dark feelings during the day and nocturnal nightmares. Mary. A tear ran down his cheek, accompanied by another, becoming a gentle flow of soft ache.

She played the piano and could take over as organist when needed. A real talent. He could still hear the music she played, had a vision of the enjoyment she felt and gave. His great regret was that he could not play an instrument.

Come on lad, pull yourself together! This isn't going to get that book written, the one you promised Mary you would write when you retired. Books flood out of people in anger, regret, inspiration, bouts of creativity. Amazon is littered with the sweat of many brows, many of which will never be read. Good reason to give up before you get started then? Yes and no.

What else burns on the bucket list? The thought of his late father's 1950 Ford V8 Pilot Limousine cheered him up. Lovingly covered and waiting challengingly in a storage unit on an industrial estate at Longmire, near Banbury. For almost five years. He had promised himself that one day he would make the effort to restore it. Well not exactly restore as it was fairly immaculate and had only covered 16,000 miles. Use it was more accurate. Time had been the problem but now he had time. Buckets of it.

Finished in dark royal blue with blue and linen interior.

Open a door and smell the leather! He had driven it for Angela and Beth's weddings, jumping out at his church in his robes and dashing to the altar past Mary's happy face. Mary. He checked himself and concentrated his thoughts on the V8. Adding electronic ignition was part of his plan. Soon he would make a start! The vision of overalls and spanners and oily rags beckoned enticingly.

He had a book to write first. He guessed he was not the first to want to write in retirement. He had made notes, vague plans tossing in his mind like a broken tumble drier. Tossing round and round, doing nothing. Got to make some heat lad, stop faffing around making excuses. There would be heat, oh yes, precious feathers ruffled.

He moved from the cosy lounge into the small dining room which was now a study. Nothing like the size of studies he had had in vicarages but this one was his, a fully paid-up member of the creative writers' club. That's a point, how much truth should go in? Mary had hoped for a positive journey with happy anecdotes, a sort of glorious autobiography.

He didn't see it like that, feeling it should be a journey yes but with warts and all. It would be controversial, open to inter-pretation which would create the heat. There is heat and heat. Flames when fanned can quickly get out of control. Good, bring it on!

The desk almost filled the study. Doug leaned back in his battered leather office swivel chair and stared at the photos of Mary, their children and grandchildren on the wall.

He nudged the chair back from the desk and it hit the wall behind. Felt a bit embryonic, safe and warm but confined. He concentrated his mind and ideas started to flow, slowly at first.

Then faster and faster, almost overwhelming in their intensity.

He leaned forward and opened an empty Word document on his laptop. Time to get something down on paper. He typed for half an hour, read and re-read, nodding. Typed for another half an hour. It was coming into shape. His aim was to question his thirty-six years of ministry, critically assess what he had achieved, if anything. He found more questions than answers. This did not surprise him but was unsettling. Surely a clergyperson should be the most likely person to at least claim to have all the answers. Perhaps that is the problem.

He threw his reading glasses on the desk, pulled on his overcoat and the woolly hat and scarf Mary had knitted. He needed fresh air, to stretch his legs, clear his mind.

He went down the narrow path to the front gate, walking down the pavement towards the village. Then turned abruptly in the other direction. Nobody knew him in the village, he was just a newcomer. He wanted to keep it that way. People shy away from dog collars like the plague. When he did meet villagers he wanted to be the guy who recently retired, like so many of them, only revealing minimalistic bits of his career and past life.

He smiled. Should he say he was the *Man from U.N.C.L.E*, this seemed to fit in with Man of God, in a weird sense. Ex-manager of a shop sounded convincing. If pressed as to what that involved, he could simply comment a lost and found shop. They could make what they would of that without further explanation.

He pondered why he wanted or needed to hide his background. He did not need to, he just wanted to. Not to be bothered with strange looks, minds already made up with images of the cloth instead of the man. To be free. Ha, free! *Man is born free but is everywhere in chains.* Rousseau got that right.

If he was to do a lot of walking alone, perhaps he should get a dog. Company. Not a bad idea. Find an animal shelter and give a dog a second chance. For both of them.

He had visions of a faithful friend lying at his feet while he wrote the book, gazing admiringly up at him, giving inspiration and listening to his questions. Walking by his side, sitting on the sofa together cuddling and comforting. He liked the thought and decided to put it top of his to do list.

They had had a dog when the children were small, a white Scotty called Jock. They got him as a pup and he lived to the grand age of fifteen and gave much pleasure, though endless tears when he passed away. Why does love always have to pass away? Grief is the form love takes when someone we love dies. Oh to be in the presence of the one we love just one more time.

Mary, Mary, how long will this grief last, does it ever end, or does it dissolve into some more palatable existence. All the comforting words he had said to the bereaved at funerals seem so trite now Mary, so empty, so inadequate, though always sincere.

Snow was lightly falling as Doug arrived at the animal rescue centre. He was welcomed by the manager and shown the over-full kennels with so many hopefuls. Another happy decision, hope again for the adopter and the adoptee. A new life. The dogs jumped at the railing to their pens, trying to push head and paws through the gaps. Me human, me, look at me!

Playing God again eh, will it never end. Why couldn't he take them all home. He remembered someone once saying that the one for you would stand out from the crowd. Sadly it did not. He walked slowly up and down the line of railings again, his heart heavy and disappointed.

Then he saw a Golden Retriever leaning against the rear wall of its pen, dejected and withdrawn. Seemingly to have given up on life, lost all hope with no faith in humans. It glanced in his direction as he passed, then stared back at the wall. He paused thoughtfully.

The kindly manager noted his hesitation, and she explained the dog was a four-year-old bitch who had been abandoned when her owner died. The family did not want her and had brought her to the kennels, dumped was the word she used.

Usually Doug always considered carefully before making decisions, mulled over the pros and cons before acting. He asked the dog's name and was told Ruby. It was a Tuesday.

'Well Ruby Tuesday, shall we go home?' he muttered. 'It seems we have a lot in common'.

The kennel lady liked the look of Doug as soon as she met him. The deep expressive eyes under the white hair displayed a man to be trusted.

'OK Mr Spencer, I think you are well suited. She is yours. Good luck to you both'.

Paperwork completed, discussion about Ruby's likes and dislikes done, and a little to his surprise he found himself leading her to his car. He opened the tailgate of his estate and paused. Closing it again he opened the front passenger door and beckoned Ruby to jump in. After a glance at him, a sniff at the seat, then Doug again she jumped in, curling up as though claiming her regular place.

He closed the door gently so as not to startle her, walked round and got into the driving seat.

'Well Ruby Tuesday, here we go. Day One. Let's go home and get something to eat'.

Chapter Two

The next few days passed quickly; they walked and walked, played ball in the garden, had long one-sided conversations. Until Doug woke up one morning with a start. Ruby jumped off the bed as he threw on some clothes and dashed down to the clickie room. Oh no, that never ends well.

Doug stared at the blank screen. Ruby lay at his feet. She had got used to the squeak of his office chair as he shuffled backwards and forwards, wondering why he looked for ages at this bright light thing on his desk, sighing deeply. Ah, something is happening. Walkies? No chance.

Surely inspiration had to kick in soon, he had to type something, Christmas was coming. He had written a few pages but deleted them. He patted Ruby and his mind cleared. She jumped as his hands flew to the keyboard.

He seemed to be clicking for quite a while, the hands on the wall clock had moved round half a circle. The chair groaned as he leaned back to survey his efforts. Ruby opened her eyes, then closed them again. Boring.

He read thoughtfully, leaning forward intently at times when something caught his eye. Not a bad effort. Time for a coffee and a stretch. Ruby followed him into the kitchen with an expectant look, satisfied with a treat.

He drank the coffee he had just made, leaning against the work surface. He wanted to say something about churches and how many fail to attract people. What are the problems? Why do they reach the so-called saved but turn off the majority?

This was a discussion he had had with Mary many times. She would not approve of his words, she always seemed happy with their clergy life; the moving, the disagreements in parish life. She could pour oil on troubled water, bring out the positive in situations. Everyone loved Mary, even when they were at odds with him.

He had to ask himself why he was writing - was it bitterness, frustration or simply pain? The pain of loss, being alone. On balance he did not think so. Well, partly maybe. He must be clear in his mind about this, not open up old wounds because he was hurting. Clarity would not come out of confusion.

He had decided the best way was to write and then edit. Keep re-drafting until he was sure what was on the screen was what he really wanted to say. Anyway, would anyone bother to read it? Why ruin a quiet life by stirring up matters best left unspoken? No, that is the coward's excuse for inaction. Ideas which seem to attack, rock the status quo, must be stated and defended with passion. Some will applaud, then forget. Those feeling aggrieved will never forget.

He drained the mug and looked at Ruby. So content, lying

silently on the floor, concerned only with food and walkies. And affection.

'To continue or not to continue, Ruby. Aye, that is the question'.

She raised her eyes a little to look full in his face but he could not read her reaction. She may not understand the words but she seemed well aware of his turmoil. That has got to be worth another treat.

He returned to the clickie room and sat down, looking hopefully at the screen. He jumped as he questioned whether he had remembered to save his work. If not, did it matter? Perhaps better to let it drift into cyberspace. No, he had saved it. He re-read it again and nodded slowly. Yes, this is what he wanted to say. It was taking shape.

Ruby assumed the position. Time for a nap, got to be walkies soon. Here we go again, click click click.

∝

Doug decided to venture into the village. He felt ready to meet people, and putting on Ruby's lead they strode forth. She sniffed excitedly as they walked, clearly enjoying the new experience. It should have been no more than a twenty-minute brisk stroll but took nearly an hour.

He needed the post office and as he approached, wondered if they allow dogs. As he hesitated, a lady came out and they almost collided. The usual apologies were offered and he stood aside to let her exit. He paused in the doorway, looking at the cashier behind the small counter as he pointed to Ruby with a questioning look. She nodded with a smile.

The post office was part of a quaint general store which

seemed to sell most daily commodities from newspapers to tobacco and a selection of groceries. He glanced at the front-page headline of a weekly publication The Wiltshire News.

'Vicar Thrown Out For Affair With Church Secretary'. He wouldn't be buying that. As he bought stamps he reflected that titillation sells newspapers, any uplifting events get stuck on the inner pages.

He stood on the pavement outside, looking at Ruby with a sigh.

'Think yourself lucky kidda, you live in this world but don't understand it. Join the club!'

She sniffed.

'Hey, looks like there's a café over there. Come on, let's drown our sorrows.'

He peered through the window. A sign read *Dogs welcome*. Ruby sniffed the air, picking up the pleasant waft of cake and scones with glee.

They went in and he sat at a table near the window. As he looked for a waitress, his eyes met the lady from the post office collision sitting at a corner table. He looked away, patting Ruby self-consciously.

He looked up, thinking it was the waitress. It was her, smiling down at him.

'Hello, I'm Tracey, Tracey Harrison.' She held out her hand.

'Oh, er, nice to meet you. Doug Spencer.'

He stood up. They shook hands. Hers was soft and warm.

'May I join you?'

'Please do' as he indicated the chair next to him.

'I haven't seen you in the village before. Are you a newcomer?'

'Yes, well I suppose you could say that. Fairly new.'

'I thought so. Where have you moved from?'

The waitress made a timely appearance.

'Would you like anything?' he asked politely.

'Oh, thank you, another coffee would be nice.'

He ordered two coffees and some scones.

'What a lovely dog.' She patted Ruby who growled.

'Thank you, yes she is. My Ruby.'

He felt awkward. What should he say? What did she want?

She seemed pleasant enough; softly spoken, early fifties he guessed. Her hazel eyes glowed warmly in a thin face framed by medium length dark hair.

The coffees and scones arrived.

'Would you like jam or just butter?' asked the waitress, in that bored tone of voice from repeatedly covering the same ground.

He gave his uninvited guest a quizzical look.

'Oh both please. Strawberry jam.'

She cut and buttered a scone, spreading jam from one of those annoying sealed plastic trays which he always found difficult to open. She did not.

A folded newspaper she had been carrying slipped to the floor at her feet. As he retrieved it, he noticed it was a copy of the one he had seen in the post office. He picked it up, handed it to her.

'Have you seen the front page? Just shows you'.

Shows you what? The conversation was going in a direction he did not want to go.

They talked generally for a while. He tried to convince himself that she was a pleasant lady welcoming a newcomer to the village, and that their paths may not cross again. Did he want anything more? He had his life with Ruby, he needed to write the book and the Ford V8 Pilot was waiting for his attention.

The Pilot! He really wanted to get started on that. His mother and father had lived in Abingdon all their married life, his father was a bank manager there, having begun his career in Banbury. The car had been his pride and joy and Doug had happy memories of many outings, viewing the world from the luxury of the rear seat as it flashed by.

Doug and Mary had moved several times. Starting in a parish near Cheltenham, then Coventry and finally Stoke-on-Trent. Mary wanted them to retire to Wiltshire as her parents liked the area and she had many happy childhood memories of visits.

Realising Tracey was still talking and that he had been looking at her without really listening, he wondered why his listening skills were deserting him. Throughout his ministry he had been a good listener; not simply nodding in the right places but actually hearing what people had to say and genuinely trying to help. Mary had often remarked that empathy was one of his gifts.

At an appropriate moment, goodbyes were exchanged and he retreated. Ruby seemed eager to leave, pulling on her lead as they made for the door.

The next morning they were both in the clickie room. Ruby chewed on her daily Dentastix, staring up at him as he stared at the keyboard. It wasn't blank, he had saved fifty-six pages. How many pages should he write? How long's a piece of string… a hundred, more? Keep going until you come to the end!

He sipped from a mug of strong coffee. It had not been

so much a struggle as a cathartic process. The words flowed fairly effortlessly.

Now he had time to reflect, contemplate. During his busy ministry the thoughts he was writing down had always been at the back of his mind. Uncomfortably floating around yet without focus, like a storm without an eye.

What puts people off churches, why are numbers dwindling as the faithful pass on? The younger generation do not seem to find what they are seeking in beautiful buildings. Was the beauty an attractive addiction which masked the truth instead of proclaiming it?

Decline has a reason. To bury heads in the sand and hope for the best is doomed to failure. Had he been part of the problem, merely maintaining the status quo? Plodding on regardless, eyes wide shut, part of the system, afraid to challenge the great machinery which was slowly grinding to a halt.

Addressing charges of hypocrisy are a defence mechanism, fending off thinking about the unthinkable. In all the stress of modern life, with social media continually forcing opinions and creating more stress, precious little space to think about 'religion'. So don't bother. Unless it is ingrained from childhood, becomes a way of life. Security in an increasingly insecure world.

He clicked back through his words so far. Had he got this across? Ruby seemed to nod. What next? He picked up the worn leather Bible on the desk and thumbed the pages. He paused at the *Acts of the Apostles*. Parts of chapter two were heavily underlined in red.

Verse 37: 'Brethren, what shall we do?' Verse 38: And Peter said to them, 'Repent, and be baptized every one of you of in the name of Jesus Christ for the forgiveness of your sins; and you shall receive the gift of the Holy Spirit'.

He read for the umpteenth time about the brotherhood of believers who had all things in common, sold their possessions and goods and distributed them to all, as any had need. And day by day, attending the temple together and breaking bread in their homes... and the Lord added to their number day by day those who were being saved.

So simple, yet so complicated. Why bother with a church building at all, why not meet in a pub?

Ruby rolled over and he tickled her tummy. Was it all about tickling tummies, making people feel good whilst living under the oppression of man-made theology? Endless liturgies. Endless night.

Many people seem to have concluded they show their love for God by attending church services. For some reason, they think that makes God happy. Why? Jesus never talked about attending services, although church can be a good container to start with. Not the be all and end all.

In an age of questions and rebellion, doubt challenging history, it was all falling apart. What used to be accepted without too many questions as simple truth, is in the complexity of today's life being thrown out with the bathwater.

Good thoughts, he typed furiously. Perhaps he should record his thoughts, use his mobile 'phone. His ideas came faster than he could type. Who would do the necessary transcribing though? He couldn't.

Mary could. Would she have wanted to? She would gladly have done the practical work but would not have liked what she was hearing and typing. She would have questioned why he wanted to say these things, why poke the animal which had been their life together. Her opinion would have been that his words might cause upset and confusion.

He remembered words he had heard during his theological training, words which still had a big impact on him. 'No growth without conflict'. Mary always shied away from conflict of any kind, it was her nature. She was not a coward, far from it but she wanted to encourage people rather than cause them pain.

He had once been on a 'plane when the pilot announced 'Ladies and gentlemen, we are entering an area of turbulence. Please fasten your seat belt.' His whole life had been turbulent, perhaps it was time to unfasten his seat belt and fly free.

Was his pain making him want to poke a stick into the cage of tradition and respectability? Maybe. He preferred to think of it as trying to clear his confused mind, finally to lay the past to rest. And in so doing find some sort of peace. For his future. He must have one...

Chapter Three

There was a knock at the front door. Leaving the desk, he looked through the window. Oh no, that Tracey woman. How the heck… then he remembered their café encounter and telling her roughly where he lived. Ruby growled.

'I hope I'm not interrupting anything?' she smiled.

He wanted to reply yes, go away but welcomed a break from writing.

'No, come in'.

He led her into the lounge. She sat on the two-seater settee. He sat on the matching chintz armchair. If they stretched their arms they might just about touch the walls. He waited. Oh, better offer a drink.

'Cup of tea? Or coffee?'

'Tea would be nice, thank you."

'Milk? Sugar?'

'Just milk please."

Ruby had followed him to the front door, then into the kitchen and stayed there. He returned with two mugs of tea.

'Sorry about the lack of ceremony, the china's still packed away somewhere.'

'No problem, I'm a mug person most of the time.' She raised her mug in salute.

Silence. What did she want?

'How are you settling in?'

'Oh, not too badly thanks. Getting there.'

'I suppose there is a lot to get used to?'

Interesting. He thought back to their last meeting. He had not revealed much in the general conversation, only where he lived. Roughly. Fair dos, there was only his cottage in that area so it did not take a genius to work it out.

She cradled the mug in both hands and observed him over the rim. His beard could do with a trim. He would look younger and his handsome features would be more noticeable.

He sipped, feeling bewildered. You either like people or you do not, sometimes reserve judgement. He liked her.

She asked questions and to his surprise he did not find this intrusive. It was as though she was genuinely interested. He was however determined that his past should remain private, he had never been one to reveal much about himself. A career of listening had taught him that basically all others want is to be heard and understood. For themselves. That was his stock in trade and he understood the rules.

'There's an animal show just outside the village next week. Thursday, all day. Weather permitting. I was wondering if you might like to come, Ruby would enjoy it.'

That's worth considering. Ruby must get fed up being inside

with him most of the time. Maybe he should get out and meet people.

'Yes, that sounds good' he found himself saying.

'Good. I have a leaflet here with the details. Somewhere.'

She rummaged in her large flowery handbag, pulling out a wad of leaflets and gave him one.

'Dave Harrison is the organiser, you'll see his name at the bottom. He's my ex. This show is about the only thing in common we have left' she added in a matter-of-fact tone.

'Oh, right. Thank you. Yes, I think we'll be there' was his comment as he glanced through the leaflet, trying to process what she had just said.

He glanced at Ruby sitting in the kitchen doorway. She turned her head away.

Thursday morning was clear and bright and Doug felt good as he got out of bed and looked out of the window.

'It's gonna be a good day,' he announced to Ruby. 'A bright sunshiny day.'

They set off towards the village, the show being in a field on the other side. People were moving in that direction so they followed. Having paid the entrance fee, Doug allowed Ruby to lead him onto the show field. She scampered and sniffed, happy to explore the new smells as she pulled on the lead.

He looked round, not many people but it was early and the show had only been open half an hour. Many stalls were still being set up. He saw Tracey talking with a man about her own age. Was this Dave? They appeared to be getting on well but she had said there was no animosity and no children to argue over.

Ruby was pulling him in another direction, following a couple with a black Boxer. He tugged gently and reluctantly she followed as he headed towards Tracey. Anyway, she had spotted the supposed Dave, or rather an Alsatian sitting by his side.

As Ruby pulled, Doug tried to hold her back, filled with ambivalence. Did he want to pursue this upcoming event, if so why. Every step forward was a step into unknown territory. Not too late to turn around, walk away. He had been seen but could wave and walk. Backwards. Is that what he wanted, to retreat to his empty life?

Tracey approached with her warm smile. He allowed Ruby to pull him, as she headed for the Alsatian.

'Hello. Nice to see you. Come and meet Dave. He's brought Ludo of course.'

Ruby and Ludo sniffed each other, tails wagging. Doug moved her lead to his left hand as he shook hands with Dave. So it *was* Dave. Looked alright, slightly older than Tracey, quite good looking. Smartly dressed in a modern style, a flat country cap covering well-groomed brown hair. Bit like a photograph in a country magazine. The local squire.

They chatted together, Dave remarking on Ruby's vitality and keen instinct. Ludo's qualities were expounded with the hopeful comment that he would win a prize.

Dave said he should do the rounds and moved away, Ludo trotting at his side. Ruby excitedly wanted to follow and took some controlling.

Tracey tried to read Doug's expression but there was none.

'There you are, you've met Dave' she said after a couple of minutes, feeling her way.

'Indeed I have. Seems a pleasant enough guy.'

'Oh he is. He's a damn good architect, very successful. Won a couple of prizes recently.'

That's nice, dog prizes and architectural prizes. What more is there in life he told himself sarcastically.

As they walked slowly round the show looking at the stalls, she explained that Ludo had always been Dave's dog and it was natural for them to be together after the divorce. She was fond of dogs but could not come between them, enter into a popularity contest. Anyway, she had kept the house.

They stopped at the refreshment marquee and sat at an outside table. Doug went in and after a few minutes appeared with teas and slices of homemade cake on a tray, Ruby still attached to his wrist. He had thought for a moment about leaving her with Tracey but had sensed canine reluctance. Perhaps she didn't want to be left, after all they spent so much time together.

He didn't feel awkward now, more relaxed. Could be what he needed, fresh air and company. His tensions seemed to be unwinding.

'You keep your cards close to your chest' she suddenly commented, 'bit of a dark horse.'

'Am I? He paused, cup halfway to the saucer. 'Not much to tell really. Unless you like classic cars.'

'You know, funnily enough I do. I have a mint '63 MG Midget, drive her all the time. Maybe you'd like to see her sometime?'

Images flashed across his mind. Small two-seater sports car produced by MG from 1961 to 1979. 948cc. Must be a Mark 1, they started producing Mark 2s in 1964. Nice little two-seater sports car but he preferred the Austin-Healey

'Frog-eyed' Sprite, more character. Of the same era.

Thinking about classic cars always cheered him up. He'd had a love relationship with them over the years, had owned a few beauties. One at a time, being poor as a church mouse he had to restore one and then sell before re-investing. The Pilot came into his thoughts and he smiled. Soon and very soon.

'Love to. Always up for looking at a classic.'

'Fantastic. She's in white. OK, let's do it. Next week. Give me your number and I'll ring you to make a date.'

Chapter Four

She rang as agreed, giving her address. An estate of detached houses on the outskirts of the village. Tomorrow was the day.

As he sat in the clickie room, Ruby in her usual place, he paused and leaned back. There seemed less anger in the prose lately, more contentment. Somehow more balance. Could what he had written so far have been a product of his feeling of failure, channelling his disappointment with churches into a vendetta? Making a mountain out of a molehill.

Then he remembered the many comments of disappointment and despair he had heard over the years from non-churchgoers. They can't all be wrong. The chorus of the disaffected. Seeing handbags and glad rags, mitres and robes. Power and money, bums on pews.

'OK kidda, here we go. Let's go look at this car.'

Ruby jumped up with a sniff and followed him to the front

door. He glanced in the hall mirror as he passed. Hair in place, beard looking presentable. Different clothes for a change, oh yes, like the jumper.

It was a twenty-minute brisk walk to the housing estate. A road turned off to the right just before the village and wound into what he called a posh estate. Three and four bedroomed detached houses for professionals. With double garages. Wow, that's living in style, two cars.

Following the road as it branched into bird names, he came to Birch Grove. Three bedroomed detached. For the smaller family. Such as one couple and a dog. He rang the doorbell of 38.

It was opened immediately and there she was, dressed in a thick cardigan, slacks and boots. She wore a flowered headscarf. Ruby sniffed and backed away.

'Hi Doug. Good, you found me. Come in for a drink and then I'll show you Gemma.'

She stepped aside and they entered the long hallway. She indicated a door to the right, leading into a bright lounge with bay window at the front and patio doors to the rear.

He sat on the leather settee and let Ruby off the lead. She circled the room restlessly.

'Tea or coffee?'

Tracey returned with two mugs of coffee, then went back to the kitchen for a plate of biscuits. The latter attracted Ruby's attention and she sat motionless in expectation. Tracey nodded at Doug's questioning look and he gave Ruby a Hobnob, first breaking it in two.

'No crumbs please' he admonished, adding 'Good girl' as both halves disappeared in a flash.

They chatted, drinking coffee and nibbling biscuits, another two entering Ruby's open mouth. Then the moment arrived.

'Ready for a spin? Lovely day for it. The garage is this way.'

She led through to the kitchen, grabbing a thick scarf from a clothes rail in the hall. She opened a door at the back of the kitchen, leading into a garage with the gleaming Midget parked in the space nearest the door.

'Say hello to Gemma' she said proudly as he looked round her.

'Mmm, nice one. Very nice. Can I have a look at the engine?'

She opened the bonnet to reveal a very clean engine compartment, which Doug inspected thoroughly.

'Twin SU carbs, lovely.'

'HS2s' she replied in a matter-of-fact tone.

He was impressed.

'Wow, you certainly know your stuff!'

'Learned from my father. He was an MG enthusiast.'

He examined the bodywork, feeling certain areas.

'No filler, all original metal. She's certainly in pristine condition. And the upholstery is unmarked.'

'Jump in, let's go for a spin.'

The top was down. She backed Gemma into the driveway and opened the passenger door.

'What about Ruby, shall I keep her on my knee?'

'Nope, she should fit OK behind the seats. She'll still be near you.'

With some coxing and much sniffing, Ruby jumped into the tight space behind the seats.

Tracey expertly wound round the entrance road, and on reaching the main road put her foot down. The light wind blew in their faces, Ruby's nose aloft and twitching.

The days that followed were full of car tours and picnics, chats and revelations. Doug felt completely relaxed, happier than he had felt in a long time. His visits to the clickie room became quite infrequent.

It was some two weeks since their first forage in Gemma.

They had so many common interests. Except religion. Tracey was a committed agnostic. At least she wasn't an atheist, in his opinion that might be a bridge too far. He would have found it difficult, if not impossible to have a close friendship with a person who lacks belief in the existence of God.

As evening fell he found himself strolling round the garden with Ruby, his mind doing somersaults. Was theirs a close relationship? Was it going anywhere? Did he want it to, and if so where? Or was he on the rebound, searching for the paradise he had lost.

A car pulled up at the gate. He wasn't good on modern models, they all look the same. No character. It was an estate car similar to his but newer. And more expensive.

Dave saw him and jumped out. Doug had an uneasy feeling. What was this all about…

They stood each side of the gate, clearly wanting to keep a physical barrier between them. Dave's face was a mixture of hail fellow well met with a slight twinge of insincere concern that Doug found unsettling.

'Hi Doug. I was hoping I'd catch you in. Got a couple of minutes?'

Doug paused to reply as his mind raced with possibilities. Was this wise, but how could he refuse. Tell him to buzz off.

No, better with the devil you know or rather the one you don't know, and don't want to. He had to hear what the man wanted to say but from a safe distance.

'Yes'.

Very noncommittal. Not rude but adequate under the circumstances. What did he expect, to be invited in for coffee? No man, spit it out and be gone. Ruby tilted her head sideways with a questioning look.

'OK. I'll come to the point. You and Tracey seem to be getting close'.

None of your damn business. Your bus has gone. Time for someone else standing at the bus stop to get on board and see where the journey leads. Doug made no reply.

'Well look pal, I think you need to be aware of something, a bit of advice'.

Stop right there! He hated being called 'pal' and didn't want advice. But Dave was going to give it anyway.

'I hear you used to be a vicar'.

Oh no thought Doug, this really is going somewhere I definitely do not want to go. Where did he get that piece of information?

'You may or may not know that Tracey is a reporter for the Wiltshire News. Sort of scoop journalist, digging out stories, that kind of thing.'

No, he didn't know.

'Well, she wrote that article about the local vicar who got thrown out for shagging his parish secretary. Caused a big kafuffle round here I can tell you.'

He paused for a reaction. None. The lack of reaction spurred him on.

'She is sniffing around for a bigger story. Thought you should know.'

Silence. Eventually Doug spoke. Slowly, patiently, without emotion.

'OK Dave, now you've told me. I hope you feel better. Have a nice evening.'

He turned towards the cottage, Ruby faithfully following at his heels.

Dave stood looking after them for a couple of minutes, shrugged and returned to his car. As he engaged first gear he shook his head, glanced in the rear-view mirror and was gone.

Stopping at the front door, Doug paused with his hand on the handle. Did he want to go in or did he need fresh air? He clipped on Ruby's lead and headed for the gate.

They walked for miles. It was dark when they arrived back at the cottage. His mind was still whirling but they couldn't walk all night. Anyway, that may not bring a solution. If there was one.

Time for Ruby's tea. He went into the kitchen and automatically filled her bowl, then the water bowl. Then he filled the kettle and made a coffee. He did not feel like eating, bit sick.

Waiting for the kettle to boil he stared out of the window. All he saw was his reflection. You fool. You've been conned lad, buttered up and toasted. It was not a pleasant feeling.

He took the coffee into the lounge and slumped wearily into his chair. Ruby sensed all was not well and lay at his feet, staring up at his drawn face.

No fool like an old fool. One born every minute. Should he keep seeing her but be very guarded? Or break it off. Break what off. It was only a friendship and they usually come to an end, in the end. True, some seem to be eternal, the deep relationships. Most have a limited life span and gradually peter out. Some stop abruptly with no explanation. Some without apparent reason.

He did not like loose ends. Too much baggage to store away which pops up at unexpected moments. There had to be honesty, cards on the table before the end could be accepted and put away. Otherwise, the jack-in-the-box could jump out when least expected.

He had to talk with her. If only for one last time.

Chapter Five

The night was restless. He drifted in and out of sleep; getting up, pacing, drinking tea, muttering and unsettling Ruby.

By dawn he had made a decision. Get away, break out. Visit the Pilot and make a start. Forget everything in a labour of love.

Ruby danced around as he threw some clothes into a travel bag. How many days? Who cares, let's just get out of here.

He found his overalls and put them in the back of the estate with his toolbox.

Soon they were on their way to Longmire. He remembered a pub there that did B & B and hoped it was still open. The Crown? Then to the unit on the industrial estate and get started!

He thought about Tracey and what he had been told about her. He had calmed down to some extent but was still hurt. So many unanswered questions. Would he ever know the truth? He was determined that he would find answers, but not now.

They were soon on the M4. Ruby had her nose out of the

passenger window which was slightly open. This was exciting, new smells, new friends to meet. Her tail wagged in time to the sounds from the engine.

Traffic was not too heavy and they made good time.

The Crown was still open and Doug checked in. No problem with Ruby, dogs welcome. She sniffed the double room and was satisfied. An Airedale Terrier had stayed a week or so ago and his scent was still wafting on the easy chair and most of the carpet. Heaven. She watched Dad unpack his bag, pleased he had left those smelly overalls in the back of the car. Clean enough but still stinking of that oil stuff. Yuck.

Doug sat on the edge of the bed and looked at her.

'Tomorrow kidda I'm taking you to see something really special. You'll love it like I do, wait and see'.

She rolled over, yawned, and fell asleep, wagging her tail contentedly as the scent on the carpet induced sweet dreams.

Doug drove out of the pub car park and headed west. He put his left hand in his jacket pocket, feeling for the Pilot and storage unit keys. Relax, they were there. It was five months since he had been to the unit. He went there when he felt down, needed comfort and a sense of purpose. A lot had happened. Ruby had come into his life, very much on the plus side. On the down side… push those thoughts away, they were of the immediate past and future, not for today.

His hand trembled as he put the key into the padlock securing the unit door. He was ready in his overalls. He flung the door open and there she was! Carefully removing the dust cover, he walked round the beauty inspecting every inch. Perfect.

He sat in the driving seat and put his hand lovingly on the column gearstick, imbibing the luxurious smell of leather. Would she crack up or would the battery need charging? As he turned on the ignition, lights on the dashboard lit up. Looking good. He pulled out the choke and cracked her up. He cheered as she roared into life.

Doug worked all day connecting the new electronic ignition system with the parts he had brought with him. Pausing only for a couple of coffees from a flask and sandwiches The Crown had kindly provided. Ruby walked around but mostly slept, waking abruptly when a piece of sandwich was offered.

As he eventually pulled off the overalls, he winced in pain. Must have twisted something with all that bending. Getting old lad, better try to walk it off.

It was like going back in time as he walked through the industrial estate, Ruby trotting at his side. Amateur mechanics were working on their daily transport but mainly classics and motorcycles. One guy had obviously been repairing his classic motorcycle and was riding up and down, running through the gears and roaring the motor. Needs a new silencer mate if you're prepping for an MOT.

It was a bright Spring late afternoon, perfect for a stroll. They walked down a lane and turned into a field. He remembered there was a river somewhere close but was unsure of the direction.

There it is! As they approached Ruby ran off, scrambled down the riverbank and gratefully lapped the cool water. As he sat on the bank watching, he noticed a dilapidated little caravan nestling under a huge oak tree further down the river.

He set off slowly in that direction, his curiosity getting the better of him. Ruby bounded up the bank and followed. What's

Dad up to now, hope it's not noisy, had enough of that.

As they approached two figures leapt out through the door. They stood side by side, arms folded in defiance. Ruby sniffed ferociously, this was good smells.

'You from the council? We ain't movin' exclaimed the young man, glaring into Doug's face.

'No, we bloody ain't' echoed the girl.

Doug was taken aback. He reassured them that he was not from the council and saw their bodies relax. They put their hands in the pockets of their dirty jeans. They looked like two peas in a pod, dirty pullovers and heavy boots. This was clearly their residence.

Introducing himself as a visitor to the area out for a walk, they started to talk. Rapidly, with a childlike naivety, often cutting over each other in their need to talk.

They all sat on the grass, Ruby sniffing the luxurious doggy smells. Good find Dad. Thelma's matted fair hair hung over her face. Wally's long dark hair was disheveled and straggly. Uncertain whether he was growing a beard or not, probably just unkept bum fluff.

They had met at the children's home where they had been placed. Both had been in care as their new stepmothers did not want them in the family. They had run away together and kept under the council radar until they reached the age of sixteen.

Instinctively Doug liked them. Rough around the edges but hearts of gold. They were intelligent but clearly their lack of education had left a mark. They certainly had no difficulty in expressing themselves, often in colourful language.

As they made a fuss of Ruby, Wally explained that they were on probation for shoplifting. They liked their probation officer who they saw as a father figure. Top guy, let them use the shower at the probation office before sessions and visited the caravan once a month with food and secondhand clothes. He was trying to find them a flat but that looked pretty hopeless. As was the possibility of employment.

Doug was intrigued. They did not seem to be seeking sympathy, just wanted to tell their story. A sad affair, not too uncommon but not something he had heard before. In fact his experience of life had been quite sheltered, tragedy yes, but his social group largely lived an existence of tedious suburban normality.

Was that his problem? Having ministered for so long to the same group of people, listening endlessly to problems which in the greater scheme of things were not problems but perceived need, all focus being on me and mine.

Here was a couple who in their short lifespan had encountered more of real life than the whole society of his experience put together.

Which brought him to consider his ministry and the man he claimed to represent and serve. A man who in his 33 years experienced all life's problems, felt pain and rejection and left a legacy that has lasted two thousand years. Proclaimed by a wishy-washy bunch of self-opinionated, egotistical imposters. Not all by any means, but regrettably the majority. He had been a paid-up member of the self-righteous, self-confessed pharisaical preaching pricks club.

Wow. Put that in the book! This young couple were a lightning conductor whose words were grounded in the reality of real life. No airs and graces, no excuses but telling it like it is. Respect.

He felt great compassion for them, not pity because that was not what they wanted. They just wanted to be heard, to be accepted for who they were. Without even understanding who they were.

They reminded him of something he had been reading a couple of days ago. 'Root of this connection is empathy; the result is kindness, compassion, respect, and understanding. When religion doesn't centre on this mutuality, it can become one of the toxic narratives that, in the end, dismantles self-love'.

Wally broke into his thoughts.

'Tomorrow we're going to this soup kitchen at some church. Want to come? You don't have to accept the religious crap, just pretend you're listening. It's quite a laugh and the grub's good. Fills you up'.

They looked at him with sincere warmth, perhaps recognizing a fellow traveler in need.

'Thelma's starting to think about their stuff. Me, I'm not sure. Maybe, maybe not. They're OK guys though. Sincere and all that'.

Would they spot a hypocrite? A low church retired Church of England clergyman who had spent a lifetime playing the game.

'Tell you what. You come and have a meal with me tonight and I'll think about it. How's that?'

Agreed. They knew The Crown. He offered to pick them up but they said they would walk. He was about to suggest a time, then saw neither had a watch. He suggested they came when they came, he would be waiting in the bar.

At seven o'clock Doug was sitting patiently on a stool in the public bar at The Crown, Ruby lying on the floor beside him. Would they come, he wondered as he sipped a glass of beer. He had ordered a table for three without a specific time.

He glanced at his watch. He wondered how they managed to keep appointments, whilst at the same time envying their free spirit. Time regulates society but also controls. If there was no time, no clocks, no watches then life would be chaotic. It is part of the human condition, but how interesting to meet two people to whom it meant nothing, or very little.

Or is it selfishness, relying that other people would fit in around their lives.

He must stop looking at his watch. And the large clock behind the bar. He was becoming obsessive. His glass emptied and he wondered if he should order another. No, wait until they arrive.

Tick tock, tick tock. He fixated on the second hand of the bar clock, watching it go round and round as people's lives slipped away. Seconds never to be recovered, precious moments which only become important at the point of death. Time like an ever-flowing stream... oh stop it! Before Einstein's theory of relativity, there was no philosophy about a relationship between space and time.

If he discussed this concept with Thelma and Wally they would probably nod and have their own thoughts. They may not know the terminology but would understand the concept.

At last they arrived and he was pleased for two reasons - one they hadn't disappointed him and secondly it would stop him playing silly mind games which were deteriorating in ever decreasing circles.

They spotted him and waved in tandem with smiles. As they approached the bar he shook their hand and asked what they would like to drink. As they sat on the stools Doug had saved, he ordered three beers.

The bar was less than half full, only half a dozen sat at the bar. The other customers were dotted round the tables; a few couples, mainly groups of varying size.

'Shall we take the drinks to our table' he suggested, sipping his second pint.

They followed him, Ruby bringing up the rear like a sheep dog, sniffing delightedly at their heels.

People at the other tables did not seem to notice the strange couple in their scruffy clothes, and were not close enough to sense an odour. Except perhaps the waitress whose nose kept twitching as she took their order.

Wally did most of the talking, Thelma emphasizing his words now and again. Churches are alright for them who go all the time. Not for guys like them, they didn't have the right. A closed club. Say they are open for all but if they waltzed in and sat on the front pews they'd probably get thrown out.

They talk about this bloke called Jesus who was always open and stuff, but don't practice what they preach.

Wally, you got it in one! He had eloquently summed up what Doug had in essence been trying to put into words for weeks. Doug was looking forward to the soup kitchen, his mind was made up.

Wally and Thelma ate a full meal, starter, main course and dessert with gusto. They talked incessantly even with mouth full, lighting up Doug's evening. He hadn't enjoyed an evening like this for a long long time.

Before he knew it, it was closing time. Doug insisted on picking them up the following evening for the visit to the soup kitchen. He made the excuse of not knowing the way but was anxious about turning up alone. Could be embarrassing.

He said he would call at the caravan in the early evening. Oh, could he take Ruby? Sure, a lot of the homeless guys have dogs.

Chapter Six

Doug parked as near to the caravan as possible, in fact he had discovered there was a lane which passed near to the back of it.

As he approached, he saw them sitting on the grass at the front. Same clothes, same hairstyles like nothing had changed. For them it probably hadn't, time seemed to pass them by.

They smiled and waved, stood up and fussed Ruby who ran straight to them. Dogs are good judges of character. Doug was happy to see them, in a strange way he was quite looking forward to their outing, never having been to a soup kitchen before. Not that he hadn't wanted to, the opportunity had never come up.

Driving over he had thought about what sort of church organised the events, the denomination and team. Soup kitchens took some organising; premises, food to buy in, preparation, funding, health & safety, insurance. With a dedicated team.

And where do the attendees come from, how and where do they advertise. Do they need to advertise, is it word of mouth?

As they walked to the car, Wally and Thelma chatted non-stop. They were an advertising campaign in themselves, bless them.

He had a good idea where the church was but allowed them to direct from the back seat. No problem parking nearby and within minutes they were about to enter.

That was when Doug felt butterflies in his tummy. Keep your mouth firmly closed, let the guys do the talking.

He noted the sign on the wall outside. Aha, evangelical. Down to earth, no frills, tell the gospel as they see it. This will be interesting.

The guys led him through the chapel and into a large meeting room which was already full. Ruby saw several dogs, and two cats, as she strained at the lead, tail wagging and nose sniffing wildly. Cats could be bad news?

Doug looked round. A long serving table, three side by side was at the far end and hot food was being served to a steady stream of eager souls holding plastic trays and mugs. They joined the queue. Potatoes, two veg and stewed meat in gravy. Spotted Dick for pudding, pop, tea or coffee.

They had to jostle for a vacant table, balancing a tray in one hand and plastic cutlery in the other. They had only been seated about five minutes when a young man approached.

'Hi Jim' Wally shouted above the noise, 'this is our mate Doug'.

Jim was the church pastor, early thirties, a striking Jesus lookalike. Well how the Aryan Jesus is portrayed, not the real one with dark hair and eyes. This one was blond, blue-eyed with a short blond beard, clad in jeans and white T-shirt.

He held out his hand to Doug with an angelic smile of genuine welcome.

The Douglas Emotional Radar kicked in. He was surprised to find his assessment was somewhere in the middle, edging more to like than dislike but definitely hovering around undecided. Because he was a fellow traveller, a religious leader to be treated with suspicion? Or simply fear of the unknown.

He had certainly made a big impression on Thelma and Wally. They chatted with him like they had known him for ever, laughing and joking with warm confidence. His responses showed acceptance and understanding, like he really cared for them, on a common level without judgement.

As they finished their meal which took Thelma and Wally all of five minutes despite talking incessantly, Jim turned his attention to Doug. His eyes displayed an open empathy, genuine enquiry and concern.

'Glad you could come, Doug. Hope you enjoyed the meal.'

Doug nodded with a smile.

'Very good thank you Jim. You certainly have a big following here.'

'We do, every night of the week. And growing. In a few minutes we'll have a few songs. Hope you can stay and join us.'

Doug nodded again.

'Great, hope you enjoy it. If you'll excuse me I have to get ready. Talk soon.'

He headed for the large serving table, talking with people as he went, clearing tables and throwing plastic plates and cutlery into one of several large black bin bags at the end. Other team members were doing the same.

Impressive, very impressive. Doug was in awe; the teamwork, the organisation were impeccable.

He wondered what songs they would sing, well known Christian songs or some of the new stuff. He doubted they would sing traditional hymns, more likely modern music.

Jim approached the centre microphone holding a guitar, and with a wave welcomed everyone, then broke into an upbeat version of *How Great Thou Art*. Several modern songs followed, the 'congregation' obviously knew some of the words, joining in and clapping. Some raised their arms in praise.

Doug's emotions were a mixture of admiration and some jealousy. The latter because it focused his very personal sense of failure, leaving a bitter taste. They were doing what he in his mind's eye had perhaps always wanted to do. No robes, no liturgy, no pomp and ceremony. Just getting the message out there, practically, meeting those in need right where they are.

He looked at Thelma and Wally. She was clearly moved and enjoying herself, tears forming as she sang along. Wally was more reticent but obviously interested and receptive.

After four songs Jim asked for a short time of prayer and the place fell silent. His prayers were from the heart, not over emotional but to the point as he prayed for their needs.

More songs followed, then Jim asked everyone to join in the Lord's Prayer which they all knew. Then he gave a blessing, welcoming them back to the Lord's house.

Jim unslung his guitar and moved round every table, hugging and shaking hands. Doug thought of his formal handshakes at the church door, sincere though they were but nothing emotional. His congregations did not want emotion. Maybe these folk needed emotion.

Happy clappy is often criticised for relying on emotion. Doug believed in head and heart, there had to be teaching but not all theology. There has to be place for the heart of the gospel, sermons often go way over people's heads. Ritual can be a deep void. He thought of Nietzsche's when you stare into the abyss, the abyss stares back at you. It tells you what you are made of. For many, deep theology helps to mask who you are, something you do not want to see.

Doug's turn came for a hug and he felt a strange mixture of stiffness, yet at the same time a longing which he could not comprehend. The father of Methodism John Wesley had described on reluctantly attending a prayer meeting: 'I felt my heart strangely warmed. I felt I did trust in Christ, Christ alone, for salvation; and an assurance was given me that He had taken away my sins, even mine, and saved me from the law of sin and death.'

Confusion, that most unwanted of human emotions was playing with his heart, and his head felt numb. He was staring into the abyss.

Jim gave him a card with contact details as he did to all newcomers.

As he drove the couple back to the caravan, Doug was deep in thought. Uneasy thoughts. Had he just had a Damascus experience? Scary yet preordained, one which could not be ignored.

Chapter Seven

The next morning he was having continental breakfast at a table outside The Crown. Ruby lay on the ground happily chewing a bone.

It had been a restless night, tossing and turning, staring at the ceiling, dozing then waking with a start. The events of the previous evening jingled and jangled as he tried to analyse everything, make some sense of what he had felt. Emotion again. His head apathetically processed his past ministry, trying to get things in some sort of order. It was all a jumbled mess. Was the opposite of emotion superstition? Go to church every week, say a prayer when you go to bed and it will all be alright on the night.

Jim's card was on the table beside his empty plate. Should he ring? What would he say, what did he want? Could anything be achieved apart from more confusion.

He picked up his 'phone, hesitated and put it down again.

He sat staring at it. This is getting ridiculous. He picked it up and dialled the number.

It did not ring for long, and Jim's voice answered. Point of no return.

'Hello. It's Doug here, we met last night when I came to the meal at your church.'

'Hi Doug, yes, I remember. How can I help?'

Good question. Could anyone help? Was he beyond help, just moving towards infinity like everyone else. Get a grip, face reality. Accept it and move on.

'Well, eh, I was wondering if you have time for a chat please' he found himself asking.

'Sure Doug, no problem. I'm in the church hall this afternoon doing some tidying up. You know, where you were last night. What about four ish?'

'Fine. Thanks, I'll be there.'

He rang off. Done now, no going back. Well there was actually, he could not turn up. Or go on and skate round the real issue. Or be honest. He would decide the appropriate course of action when the moment came. If it came. If it was used.

Doug walked into the hall with Ruby at his side. What was he doing, of all the stupid ideas… Jim looked up from wiping a table, waved and walked over, giving Doug a hug.

'Good to see you Doug. Shall we go into the chapel, it's more private there.'

'What about Ruby, shall I leave her here?'

'Bring her with you, God doesn't object so why should I.'

They followed Jim into the chapel, and he pulled out two

chairs at the front, placing them to face each other. But not too close.

"Well Doug, lovely to see you. How are you?'

As he sat down slowly, Doug looked into his face. His kind eyes were questioning, interested.

'Could be better I suppose. Look, before we start, whatever is said remains completely confidential, yes.'

'Absolutely. You have my word. Whatever is said here remains between you and me.'

He looked reassuringly into Doug's eyes and he felt confident, here is someone who is interested in me, understands my situation. Has been there, got the T-shirt. Literally, Jim's T-short read 'Jesus loves you'.

Doug had spent years, decades, listening to other people's problems. With no-one to open up to about his own. His overlords listened sure, but he always felt he had to be wary, guarded. Some problems, once disclosed come back to bite you. Congregational problems, church building problems were acceptable. But to go into deeper areas was a minefield. My door is always open was restricted to work issues, not for personal problems. Unless you had done something which would cause bad publicity. Then they wanted to know pronto to fix it, the transgressor being expendable.

He took a deep breath. Then it all poured out, he held nothing back, including Tracey. Jim showed no surprise, looked sympathetic.

After listening for twenty-five minutes, he said softly, 'Shall we pray brother.'

His prayer was one of the most sincere, compassionate petitions Doug had ever heard. From a very warm heart.

Jim quietly gazed at him.

'Do you feel better Doug, now you've got that weight off your shoulders? That was some heavy burden you were carrying.'

Doug did feel better, much. He began to understand the hurt and pain he had been carrying for so many years, other people's and how Mary and his retirement had tipped him over the edge.

He did not speak but Jim saw how much brighter he looked, his face had more colour and in a way he looked younger than last evening. His restless eyes were calmer.

'I'm here to listen. You don't need advice, you don't need me to say anything. All you needed was a friendly ear.'

At last Doug felt able to reply.

'Yes, you're right. Thank you for listening, I really appreciate it.'

'I hope, and pray that things start to fit into place now. So you can enjoy your retirement, you've got a lot ahead of you my friend.'

They sat in silence for a few moments. Then with a smile of gratitude, he gave Jim a big hug and left with Ruby who had slept through it all.

∝

Time to go. Back to reality. First a ride in the Pilot. And say goodbye to Thelma and Wally.

Ruby had come to love the roar of the Pilot, especially as it made Dad so happy. She lounged on the passenger seat, fascinated by his constant movement of that lever thingie, whilst moving his left foot up and down at the same time. When they went straight on he didn't do this and she was disappointed. She pushed her nose through the partly open window and sniffed the air as it rushed past.

Doug drove into the yard, stopping outside the storage unit. He left the engine running, opened the doors and drove in.

Ruby sat up as he killed the engine, she knew what was coming. Doug opened her door.

'Come on kidda, time to go. For now.'

Soon they were walking across the field towards the caravan. He hoped they would be in, should be as it was late morning. Probably still in bed.

They were up and about, up at least, playing cards at a rickety table, perched on two upturned logs. As Doug and Ruby approached they waved, cards in hand. They put the cards down on the table and made a fuss of Ruby who was delighted to see them.

'Hi guys, How you doing?'

'Not bad, same as usual,' replied Wally with a shrug.

'Wally might have a job. Cleaning cars at one of them drive-in places. Money's not bad.'

'Yeah, Bob the Probo told me about it. He knows the boss,' Wally added.

'That sounds great. Hope you get it Wally'.

'And I might have a cleaning job, some offices. Evenings'.

Doug wondered if Jim knew the boss of the cleaning firm, and yes, he sure did. He smiled to himself. Pastor Jim had fingers in many pies, not just holy ones. Doug felt a twinge of envy as he compared Jim's salutary ministry with his own rather ineffective efforts. He knew if he talked to Jim about this, he would say that you Doug have set many things in motion that you will never know about this side of heaven.

He asked if they had eaten to which they shook their head.

'Come on, I'll treat you to lunch. You can't start work on empty stomachs.'

He walked them to his estate car, asking where they wanted to go. McDonald's was the unanimous reply. He had never driven through a MacDonald's Drive Thru and quite enjoyed the experience. He drove into the countryside and they sat in a peaceful lane, munching double cheeseburgers and fries, drinking cans of coke. Ruby was ecstatic as she was constantly fed pieces of cheeseburger.

Doug looked through the windscreen as he chewed. How could he help these kids - well a few quid would help for sure but that would only be temporary. His thoughts were broken abruptly by a scream from the back seat.

'You little thieving bastard! You've been at it again.'

Wally was about to open a packet of chocolate biscuits which Thelma grabbed viciously.

'I never, I paid for 'em.'

'Liar!'

She shouted at Doug that they had been to the supermarket the previous evening to buy necessities with the little money they had. That did not include luxury items.

She turned her anger to Wally who had hunched over like a naughty child.

'You lyin' little prick. You're gonna end up in the nick if Bob hears about this'.

Bob, their long-suffering probation officer, would probably not report such a minor theft but would not be best pleased.

She hit him on the arm, glaring ferociously.

'What else you got?'

'Nuffin'.

'Liar!'

Doug did not know what to say. Silence is golden. He guessed anything he might say would be inappropriate and probably pour oil on already troubled water.

Ruby came to the rescue. She snuggled up to them both, first resting her head on Wally's lap and then Thelma's, growling softly.

'Doug, you tell him. Tell him what prison's like'.

He had not divulged anything about his background to them, and wondered why Thelma assumed he had been to prison. He had visited a prison once when one of his congregation was on remand for alleged fraud, and the experience was certainly not pleasant.

'Not somewhere you want to go Wally. You'd hate being locked up mate' he said lamely.

Thelma snorted.

'It bloody ain't, locked up all the time. But that's where you're gonna end up.'

An uneasy silence descended. Ruby licked Wally's face until he smiled. Thelma smiled when she licked her and Doug smiled into the rear-view mirror. Suddenly they were all laughing, much to Doug's relief.

'Come on, what we going to do now?'

'Go fishin', in the river' Wally offered, beaming all over his face like a child reprieved from the naughty step.

The couple had homemade rods in the caravan, and they spent an hour or so sitting on the bank without luck. Doug had only been fishing two or three times before but he understood the attraction; peace with nature far from the madding crowd, getting back to man's primeval instincts.

Thelma shared her rod with him and they laughed at Wally's intense expression and whoops of joy as he thought he had a catch.

Eventually Doug reluctantly said his goodbyes, explaining that he had to get home to do some work.

He wished them luck with the jobs and promised to visit them again soon. He pulled out his wallet and held out a twenty-pound note. They sheepishly shook their heads, until Wally took it with a mumbled thank you. Ruby gave them both a goodbye lick.

As he walked to his car, Doug wondered what work he was returning to. He did not want to think about it.

Chapter Eight

He did think about it as he drove. Backwards and forwards. Reflecting on the people he had just met, realising how lonely he had become of late.

He had no close friends; his ministry had not given him time and he had only had an inner circle of colleagues who met once a month to moan about their Bishop, Archdeacon and congregations.

Maybe he should visit the kids? Not sure how the grandkids would react to Ruby and he did not want to put her in kennels. Perhaps they would visit in the summer...

Continue the book? No, not yet. The compulsion had disappeared, no passion left. No need perhaps, had he found the answers he was seeking?

That left Tracey. That was probably over, not worth rekindling. A compulsive fling of friendship born out of need. But could he leave it there, unfinished, untidy. Would the betrayal fester, colour any future relationship? Was he being a coward, backing away from possible confrontation?

They did have something, they had clicked and not just over a love of classic cars.

He pulled into the driveway of the cottage. It looked dark and depressing. Uninviting.

Ruby had been asleep on the passenger seat and sat up as the engine stopped. Doug got out and she jumped onto his seat and followed him to the door.

He paused with the front door key in his hand, putting his bag on the ground. So, are you going to stand here all night, dithering and dallying? He opened the door and stepped into the hallway. It was dark and cold. He felt for the light switch and became marginally more at ease as the light illuminated half familiar nooks and crannies.

Get a grip man! He closed the door behind them and determinedly marched the few paces to the kitchen. Mug of tea and a sandwich would make things seem better. Ruby stood expectantly in front of her bowl, reminding him to get his priorities right.

Soon they were warm, fed and watered. They were home.

He woke in a positive frame of mind. As he threw back the duvet and sprang out of bed, Ruby watched him from the bed. Dad seems brighter this morning.

She followed him downstairs into the kitchen and kept an eye on him as she ate her breakfast and he thoughtfully drank his morning coffee. Hope we're not going to spend hours in the clickie room, oh no, not again.

Doug reached for his 'phone on the worktop and hesitated. Was this a good idea? Maybe, maybe not. Only one way to find out.

Tracey answered after four rings. She sounded surprised.

'Morning Tracey. I think we need to talk.'

There was a pause as she considered the request. She had thought a lot about him and why Dave had ratted on her. Dave only shared what he wanted her to know.

'Well, I suppose we do need to clear things up. And I do owe you an explanation. It isn't what you think.'

You don't know what I think, I don't even know myself. But we do need to clear the air, see if there is a way forward.

'So let's meet. Where are you now?'

She was working from home. He said he would be round shortly and hung up. Ruby growled.

He sat in her driveway staring at her front door. Not too late to reverse out. She had seen his car approach and opened the door. Too late now.

She stood aside as he entered the hall and they went into the lounge in silence.

They sat looking at each other, her crouched on a corner of the settee and him in an armchair.

At last he spoke.

'Well, where do we go from here? I don't understand, well I do, work. Getting a story. That's all that matters to people like you I guess.'

She looked uncomfortably out of the window. People like you, ouch.

'Yes, I do owe you an explanation. I'm sorry things worked out the way they did, and I'm sorry that you must have been hurt.'

'Well, it certainly looks like you used me, deliberately got to know me to get a story. To sell your rag and make a name for yourself. Pretty cheap if you ask me.'

She looked at the floor. He's right, it was a cheap shot. It did start like that, before she got to know him. But then something changed, he became a person not a news item.

'OK, cards on the table Doug. I did see a story, a follow-up to the local vicar who got thrown out.'

He interrupted.

'Ah, you thought I might have some useful secrets, poke around in my closet and see what falls out. Nice one.'

No, not nice. Pretty despicable in fact. How could she know she would get to like him, have feelings. Oh this is hopeless, how could she even begin to explain. Better not to try, only apologise and hope the sore would heal given time. There would be no quick fix, she knew that.

He talked, leaving her in no doubt that she had hurt him, deeply. He had trusted her, allowed their friendship to develop under false pretences. How could he trust her again? Once bitten…

More silence. She made coffee, glad of the break. As she handed him a mug she patted Ruby. She could not remember feeling so down.

As he sipped, a thought occurred to him.

'How did you know I was a vicar, I never told you. And how did Dave know?'

She had wondered when he would raise that point. Be honest, tell the truth, no more deception. He was worth more.

'I looked you up on the internet. You told me your name in the café that first time, when you introduced yourself. And

Dave is no fool, I must have let something slip and he probably worked it out for himself. And well, that's it.'

So that was it. The information did not make him feel any better. He had been available, another piece in her complex jigsaw. If the pieces fit, fine. If not make them, cut corners, do whatever is necessary to juggle for a story. Not his world, not the reality he had experienced. He sighed. Was his world so black and white, so concerned with truth and forgiveness and hope that he had missed the point? What was the point?

'Your world is not my world.'

As he spoke the words he thought how pathetic they sounded. Judgemental, pious, holier than thou.

'No it isn't. But because our worlds have collided doesn't mean we can't learn. If we want to.'

Did he want to? What the hell DID he want? To his surprise he crossed the space between them, sat beside her and gently kissed her lips. She responded, hugging him, passionately pulling him closer.

Ruby did not growl. She lay on the carpet watching them, her head resting between her front paws.

Chapter Nine

Doug sat with Ruby in the clickie room. He reflected on Archbishop Desmond Tutu's words 'As we share God's love with our brothers and sisters, God's other children, there is no tyrant who can resist us, no oppression that cannot be ended, no hunger that cannot be fed, no wound that cannot be healed, no hatred that cannot be turned to love, no dream that cannot be fulfilled'.

His problems seemed so insignificant in the greater scheme of things. He had new dreams, life *was* worth living. He just needed to open his eyes and believe. Not in the religious sense but in the everyday hope that everything would work out.

Wounds *had* been healed. He stared at the screen and read through some of his words. Time to draw a line. He brought up his complete manuscript and without a pause pressed the delete button. Gone.

He was moving on. He logged off and watched the screen go blank.

'Well kidda, that's it. No more living in the past, we're going to start new adventures from now on'.

Ruby was more excited with the bone she was chewing than moving on but sensed Dad was happy and crunched contentedly.

The next couple of weeks flew by. He met with Tracey several times, visited the Pilot and Thelma and Wally, took them for a ride in her.

He talked to Tracey about the Pilot and she was really interested. She knew of the model but had never seen one in real life. She asked lots of questions about the engine, and he was particularly impressed when she commented that it had twin-sheave belt pulleys, was also used in Thames trucks and was fed by a single Solex carburettor.

He invited her to see the Pilot and collected her the following week. Off they went, Ruby happy to occupy the back seat.

As they drove Doug told her about Thelma and Wally. Not Jim, that was perhaps for another time. She said that she had written an article the previous year on young people in a similar situation, and wondered if they would agree to participate in another article as the public need to hear their story. She might be able to get it syndicated to a national newspaper.

Another world, Doug thought, not his area of expertise by a long shot. That did not make it wrong, he guessed the guys might agree and it couldn't do any harm. They were the forgotten ones, he had not been aware of how they struggled until he met them.

He pulled up to the side of the unit as he would be driving her out for a test run. He felt pride in what he was about to unveil, pleased that someone was with him who would appreciate her.

Tracey stood excitedly at his shoulder as he opened the doors, letting out an exclamation of joy as he removed the dust cover.

'Oh Doug, she's beautiful!' she kept saying as she walked round and round, opening the doors and lifting the bonnet. Even inspecting the boot.

Doug smiled. 'Ready to go for a spin?'

'You bet!'

As they drove, she delicately inhaled the smell of leather, gazed at the immaculate roof lining and admired the chrome door handles and window winders.

After a few miles she asked gently if she might have a drive. Doug nodded and pulled over.

She handled the classic like a pro, changing the column gears without a sound, constantly listening to the sound of the engine, checking the dashboard instruments worked correctly as she glanced at them from time to time.

'Heaven Doug, pure heaven!' she exclaimed as she changed smoothly into second gear, accelerated and moved the lever down into top gear.

Eventually she pulled up outside the unit doors and turned to him with a disappointed expression.

'I could drive her all day Dougie, such a shame to stop. Do we have to?'

He looked into her eyes, read the pleasure of a true enthusiast.

'For now. We can always come back another day. Let's get some lunch.'

He left the estate parked across the locked doors and they walked into town. She talked about the Pilot all the way, asking questions, making favourable comments.

They ordered lunch at The Crown, agreeing on grilled plaice, homemade chips and garden peas. When the meals arrived Ruby sniffed expectantly.

Halfway through Tracey put down her knife and fork, looking at him with a questioning gaze.

'Doug, can I ask you something?'

His fork was loaded and almost at his mouth. He paused.

'OK, shoot.'

'Well' she hesitated, then the words came tumbling out. 'Look, I'm interested but it's not something I know much about.'

He imagined she had more questions about the Pilot. When she spoke again he was completely taken aback. Her tone was very quiet, almost childlike.

'Well, what sort of church are you in?'

He continued eating and she picked up her cutlery. She had given no notice of what she was about to ask, it literally came out of the blue. He sensed there was more to her question than appeared on the surface, and trod carefully. Best to answer directly and see where they went from there.

'Anglican, low Anglican.'

Clearly this had little or no meaning to her. She did not say anything but raised her eyebrows slightly to indicate 'Go on'.

He explained about the three traditions of the Church of England; high meaning anglo-catholic, middle-of-the-road being the majority and low church which is the evangelical wing.

As he spoke, he realised it was an enigma often not properly understood, even by churchgoers. Sensing her confusion he pressed on, stating that he was a member of the so-called evangelical wing, believing in biblical faith, personal conversion, and in general, the Protestant rather than the Catholic heritage of the Anglican Communion.

Sugar, he was getting in deeper and deeper. He thought it an idea to ask her what she believed, or didn't believe. She had no idea. Great, where do we go from here…

He found himself venting the frustrations he had been typing all those weeks. She listened sympathetically without interrupting.

He concluded. 'My wife Mary would have explained it all a lot better than me, she didn't have the problem I seem to have. It was all clear for Mary, she embraced it with her whole heart. No good and bad bits, for her it was all good.'

Wow, he had mentioned Mary. That was one step forward, or ten backwards. On balance he must be moving forward, surely. As she finished her meal Tracey gazed at him. She saw a sensitive man, more sensitive than she had imagined. Needy but not as in could have a psychological problem, but who needed to be listened to and wanted to be understood. Though his thoughts were not always translucent.

'I do sort of understood what you said. Not easy but maybe I'll get there one day. If you're brought up Muslim you remain Muslim. Same with Jews, Hindus and all the rest I suppose. If you're brought up in a faith you keep it, it's an identity badge you wear from childhood. Memories and all that.'

He was encouraged and thought OK, she seems to be trying to understand where I'm coming from, guess that's a positive. For the future. If we have a future, more than just a friendship.

They ate dessert in silence. He wanted to speak but found religion such a difficult subject for others. That is why he disliked the term so much.

'Moving quickly on, would you like to meet the couple I told you about this afternoon?'

'Thelma and Wally? Sure, why not.'

After lunch they walked to the caravan. They heard the shouting as soon as they were within earshot. Thelma was obviously displeased with something Wally had said or done.

Thelma saw them through a small window and dashed out.

'He's been at it again Doug! You tell him'.

Doug had warned Tracey what they might expect to find, but not quite so suddenly. He introduced her, first to Thelma and then to Wally as he hurtled out through the door. Hasty introductions to say the least.

'OK OK, calm down guys. What's up now?'

Wally had been shoplifting again, and almost got caught. Thelma was at her wits end. She would not visit him in prison, that was for sure.

To Doug's surprise and relief, Tracey took over. She sat them down and explained that she wanted to write an anonymous general article on the plight of young people such as themselves. No names. Their life story, from care to the harsh reality of life. The sort of life they found themselves in today, what the future might hold. Society needed to hear their story, to understand from a personal point of view.

When she ended they looked at each other. With shrugs they nodded. Why not, what harm could it do.

Tracey pulled her mobile 'phone from her handbag, and on obtaining their permission started recording. Questions and answers, backwards and forwards as she sat on a scruffy cushion with them on the ground, mainly arguing and poking each other.

Doug walked Ruby by the river, getting out of the way. Journalist at work.

When they returned the interview was coming to a close. The couple seemed satisfied, wanting to know which newspapers it would be in and when.

Tracey offered them forty pounds as a goodwill gesture. Thelma grabbed the notes before Wally could even react.

As they said their goodbyes and walked to his car, he looked at Tracey.

'You aren't going to get much for that story, it may not even get printed. So why the money?'

'Don't tell me you haven't given them a bob or two? Poor kids.'

Altruism. Equally guilty.

Chapter Ten

The article appeared in the Wiltshire News and was compassionate and empathetic. Told the story of two young people from difficult backgrounds, trying to make their way in a cruel world.

Doug read it again as Ruby lay beside him on the couch. He was impressed. His fear that the kids might have been taken advantage of disappeared, he should have had more faith in Tracey.

He was seeing Tracey that evening and would congratulate her. Credit where credit is due.

There was something he had been pondering for some time, and she may be able to help. He kept thinking about Jim's soup kitchen, well not really a soup kitchen, it was much more than that. Doug's vision of a soup kitchen was a mobile kiosk serving hot soup and a roll, but this was so much more. Two, even three course hot meals plus help and advice, not just words but action. Help to find jobs, even housing. And raising people's spirits, getting them singing, believing in the goodness of humanity. All at no cost whatever to the partaker.

Doug wanted to get involved in a similar project, locally. He had no notion where to start though. He bet Tracey would have a few ideas.

∝

He could not wait to see her. She was cooking a meal at her house, and Ruby's nose twitched as he carefully placed the large bunch of daffodils on the back seat.

A hug for him, a pat and bowl of food for Ruby and they were sitting in the dining room eating homemade steak pie, mashed potatoes and carrots. Tracey loved the flowers and they were in a vase on the windowsill.

She raised her glass and they toasted each other, the medium-bodied, mildly sweet Riesling going down well.

'To a sincere and creative journalist' was Doug's toast.

She smiled and raised her glass.

They chatted about this and that, mainly classic cars. After dessert she suggested Doug moved to the lounge while she made coffee.

They sat on the settee together, sipping from bone china cups. Well it isn't really a mug occasion Doug chuckled to himself.

His moment arrived.

'Tracey, do you know of any soup kitchens in the area?'

She had anticipated several possible questions but this took her completely by surprise. Surely her food was not that bad.

'Eh, well, I'm not sure there is a need round here. But there is a town about five miles away, Maidenbury, with a lot of social problems. I've seen several tramps on my travels. Why?'

He told her about Thelma and Wally taking him to the soup kitchen, omitting Jim.

'And you want to get involved in something similar round here?'

He nodded. Not with certain conviction but as a man searching for possibilities.

Tracey was concerned. This man she was liking more and more, growing deeply fond of if she was honest, this good compassionate person, was trying to find something in his retirement that he considered lacking in his ministry.

She was filled with sadness, she had little idea what was driving him but something clearly was. No, not so much driving as haunting. By what? His bereavement? No, it was more than that. An emptiness that transcended emotional loss, a void that seemed to be plunging him deeper into his very being. Underpinning his daily life, a period when he should be coming to terms with the past and seeking new horizons. Moving on.

'Are you certain this is what you want to do, Doug?'

He drank his coffee, put the cup back in the saucer and placed them on the coffee table.

'Yes. I think so.'

You think so? Oh Doug, darling Doug, thinking isn't enough. There is such a long way between thought and action.

She came to a decision.

'Tell you what, I have a friend who works in the council welfare department. Why don't I ask her what she knows, she'll be able to tell me what's happening, if you can help. OK?'

'OK. Thanks.'

The evening was over, time to go. He thanked her for a wonderful evening, praised her cooking which was top notch.

She stood at the front door and watched them both jump into their seats. She waved until the estate disappeared round the bend, walked slowly back into the lounge and curled up deep in thought on the settee.

Ruby was surprised. Here she was with Dad in the clickie room and no clicking. She lay on the floor watching as he pushed the clickie thing to one side and replaced it with paper. Lots of paper. He stared at the wall, picked up a thin bone whatsit and began drawing on the paper. He looked very happy; no frowns, no deep sighs, no strange noises coming from his mouth.

He scanned the three sheets of A4 he had already made notes on, read the list, added ever more detail. As he completed sheet four he paused.

Mentally he checked his bank account. The money left over from Mary's estate after he had bought the cottage was not a fortune, a few thousand but probably enough at least to get started. She would have given this project her blessing, have supported him all the way. She always supported him, through thick and thin. If they were still together though, would he have wanted, needed, to do this?

We mature in life. Not about growing up, some never do. It is about seeing what needs doing and having the guts to make it happen. Retirement can be a gradual shutting down or new beginnings.

He had made a list, a long list, and could not think of anything he had forgotten. When dealing with authority there would always be more, rules and regulations he had not considered. How ironic, authority having the last word about people who live outside its rules.

This had to be done right, no point in trying to cut corners. It had been done before he supposed, many times. Well, Jim had done it. Maybe he should contact Jim? Too soon, if he got stuck that would be the time.

He began another list, this time putting his initial list into categories, who should be contacted about what. This was the difficult part as he was not sure who authorised what.

Where was Tracey in all this? Did she think him mad, was she humouring him in the hope, probably expectation that he would soon lose interest? When the going gets tough, the tough get going!

He patted Ruby.

'We can do this kidda.'

He got up, saying the magic word 'walkies' and off they trotted.

He needed to see Maidenbury for himself. No point in ticking items off his list if there was no need. First he went during the day, parked in a car park and set off round the town with Ruby.

Shops are shops. Several had Closing Down signs in the window. Mothers with young kids trudged up and down the main street, shabbily dressed, not seeming to spend much money.

His overall impression was that the place had seen better days. There were no smiles, no laughter. Most of the kids were crying, pulling at their mother's arm, trying to break free. There was litter everywhere, blowing in the breeze.

Fierce-looking dogs on chains sniffed Ruby and she backed away. Stray dogs wandered around, presumably searching for food.

He saw two high-rise blocks of flats, dominating the grey skyline, which clearly needed repair. He headed towards them for closer inspection, observing the children who should have been at school, passing furtive goings on beneath the tower blocks. Drugs?

People leaning against rows of balcony walls, peering down aimlessly into the void below.

Abandon hope all ye who enter here. If this was daytime, what horrors did darkness hold?

Back at the cottage Doug felt thoroughly dejected. He had washed his hands well as soon as he got in. And his face. Was he going to do a Pontius Pilate? Pretend it would all go away, out of sight out of mind.

Oh, he knew places like that existed, he wasn't naïve. But to actually see the harsh reality with his own eyes, up close, was a revelation.

Virtually down the road. Virtual reality. His picturesque village in contrast to the hard, harsh reality of 'them'. 'The them' nobody seemed to care about. As long as I'm alright, sod 'the them'.

I either make a start he thought, or stop right here and now. Find a hobby, grow marrows, leave people to wallow on their own compost heap.

He knew he had to go back, see what night-time had to reveal.

Late that evening he drove Ruby back to the town. Only on this visit they drove the streets in the estate car. He had a disturbing feeling that walking was not advisable.

He had only driven round two streets when he thought he had died and gone to hell. Bodies were slumped in shop door-ways, huddled heaps under well-worn blankets.

Kids of all ages were running riot, charging onto waste land, back onto the streets, smashing whatever wasn't made of concrete.

As he turned for home, he passed a shop, where a group of youths, boys and girls, were kicking a bundle in the doorway.

Jesus wept.

Chapter Eleven

Back at the cottage he was more than restless. He paced up and down, flashing images flooding his mind. A concrete wall was blocking his way, mentally and physically.

He stumbled up to bed, then came down again. He grabbed his 'phone and went back up, sitting on the bed.

He did not hesitate, this seemed the natural, the only course of action. He would ring Jim. As he scrolled through his 'phone searching for the number, he glanced at the clock on the face. 23:42.

It only rang three times and the familiar voice answered with the trademark 'Jim here, how can I help?'

'Hi Jim, it's Doug. Sorry to ring so late, hope you aren't in bed'.

'No problem, just got in from the hall.' Pause. 'I've been expecting your call brother. Please go ahead.'

Doug went ahead. For almost an hour. It all poured out;

Maidenbury, his doubts, any possible way forward, rules and regulations, the whole shooting match.

'You still there Jim?' he asked anxiously.

'Sure am Doug, all the way. Listen, everything you say is true, every doubt you have is logical. Your heart tells me it understands what your head is telling you to forget. It is a battle which can go either way. Only you can make the final decision my friend.'

The line went quiet. Jim knew he was tossing things over in his mind.

'Anything else bothering you?'

Another fifteen minutes passed.

Eventually they hung up, agreeing to keep in contact. One last comment stuck in Doug's head. He was still mulling it over when he woke up in the morning.

'We can be a Daniel, dare to go into the lion's den. Or we can be a Simon Peter, run away at the Cross. Both were human. Remember Doug, Simon Peter went on from failure to do great work for his Lord'.

He drifted into an uneasy sleep, Jim's closing words echoing in his subconscious. Was this his own personal cross, something he had been able to avoid for so many decades. Clergy persons are not meant to hang on crosses, they just talk about them and physically bring them out once a year to parade round the parish.

Make your mind up time, Rev.

Tracey rang in the morning. She had some news, good news. He invited her to the cottage that evening for a simple meal.

Simple was the pinnacle of his culinary skills. She replied that she knew the limitations of his cooking, she would bring fish and chips.

She floated breezily in carrying a bulging plastic bag and a bottle of wine. She commented about his wine, laughingly calling it left-over communion wine as she wrinkled her delicate nose.

He heated plates in the microwave, poured the wine and served the fish and chips which were delicious.

He waited impatiently. They were halfway through their meal, and his curiosity was getting the better of him, when suddenly she changed the subject to focus on what he wanted to hear.

'I've had a chat with Dawn, my friend at the council, and she says there is a need for what you're thinking in Maidenbury. Big need. So much so that she wants to meet you. You have a meeting next Monday, with her and probation.'

He breathed a sigh of relief. She had been teasing him, Tracey was starting to know him too well! Dawn, new dawn, that sounds encouraging.

She laughed as he raised his glass to toast her, she hoped he wouldn't be disappointed. There was a long way to go but, well, a journey of a thousand miles starts with the first step.

She raised her glass to him. Here's to you my darling, here's to everything you hope to achieve. I am so proud of you. He did not hear her unspoken words but felt every sentiment in the warm glow of her encouraging smile.

The meeting went ahead as planned. Crowded offices in a concrete monolith. Dawn Adams had found a small meeting room and introduced herself and Mike Planter, probation officer.

She was about fifty, her face looked kind and her dress definitely not Gucci. It hung lifelessly round her ample form. Mike surprisingly was clean shaven, except for a Pancho Villa moustache which drooped at the corners. Late forties he guessed, clad in jumper and jeans with glasses which kept sliding onto his broad nose. He may have been a boxer in his youth. It was mainly his ears that told the story of beatings to both sides of the head.

They told of the social deprivation and petty crime. Doug explained that he had seen the town during the day and at night, and did not know which was worse.

They asked about his background and experience. He was honest about his background and they listened without expression. He was relieved for the absence of raised eyebrows, knowing looks or deep sighs. They seemed to accept him for what he was, a bloody do-gooder. With no experience.

When things had got as bad as they were, any helping hands must surely be welcome Doug thought, and he suspected even more monsters would lurk beneath the surface.

They were good listeners, adept at making correct assessments and decisions. They did all have that in common. When things are at rock bottom, choices are limited. Stay as they are, sink irredeemably into the mire or actually begin slowly to rise.

On a practical level they could advise on health & safety, open doors and assured him of no lack of clients. Residents of all ages would be clambering for help when they found out of his existence.

A used mobile van would be good to start with. To be in a certain place at certain times, become known and trusted. They were available for sale at one or two specialist garages, Mike knew where. The council would do an inspection and grant necessary licences.

Dawn added that no agency had any spare money. If he wanted to this, financially he was on his own.

One last point. Do not, under any circumstances hand out money, for your own sake. Keep it to meals and some grocery and toiletry items, if and when available.

Doug sat at his desk perusing the pages of to-do items. He started crossing off completed ones. The list was shrinking. Major item a catering trailer. Both Dawn and Mike had given him their work numbers, and he rang Mike. He was out on a home visit. Next time in court but third time lucky. Tomorrow they were off to look at catering trailers!

Chapter Twelve

Hectic weeks followed. No more items on his to do lists. A well-used but serviceable, and fully licensed, mobile catering unit adorned his front garden. He had given it several trials producing hot stew, tea, coffee, even hot and cold water.

The estate already had a towbar fitted, and he had practised driving up and down the road, turning corners though three-point turns needed more attention.

Ruby was very puzzled when the garage delivered the trailer, sniffing round and round this strange object taking up the driveway where Dad used to park his car. She soon got used to seeing the estate parked outside on the road, and loved scampering up and down inside the trailer when Dad was stirring pans. Though she was not sure about that thing making dark brown smelly stuff, it kept hissing at her.

Tracey had talked to villagers and several offered their help. Alice Fairbrother at the post office was first on board, and roped in a group of four volunteers. Alice's husband Gerald was choirmaster at the village church, and he recruited a small section of the choir who were willing to sing beside the trailer on its evening excursions. And being periodically reported in the Wiltshire News.

Opening night. The trailer was in place on the appointed council land. Everything was ready. As he drove the estate into a parking spot, Tracey gave him a kiss, then another. Alice leaned over from the back seat and pecked him on the cheek, to which Ruby had to join in with a lick.

Once inside the trailer, with trembling, sweaty hands Doug unbolted and swung up the large serving hatch, supported by telescopic rods.

He could see people hanging around, others streaming his way.

And Tracey, Alice and Ruby making for the entrance door.

He waved at the sky, calling 'Hey ma, if you're listening, Father Dougal here. Top of the world ma, top of the world!'

Initially he had planned Monday, Wednesday and Friday evenings from eight to eleven but demand far exceeded expectation. The people kept on coming and he could not disappoint them. Not just for food and whatever groceries he could muster, but to talk, listen to the songs and generally come together. The catering van quickly became a focal point in the town, an accepted part of the night scene.

Doug talked to Jim often, reporting on progress and seeking

advice. He needed to discuss expansion with him, where to go from here. He was going with Tracey that weekend to mull things over and make a decision. More nights? How many?

Doug felt very comfortable in his relationship with Tracey now. They thought similar thoughts, talked about the ups and downs of the project. Project. A cold word. An individual or collaborative enterprise that is carefully planned to achieve a particular aim. He preferred to think of it as a labour of love, the love job.

Interest in the village grew, more came on board. Word had spread about this retired vicar who wanted to make a difference. He was amazed that he had not needed to explain himself, his background, his hopes. Many villagers had got behind him and offered their help and support without question, had a vision of the need and were happy to get involved with whatever talents they had.

Saturday arrived and Tracey sat beside him as he drove to Longmire, Ruby stretched out on the back seat.

She knew the agenda for their visit - talk to Jim about increasing opening times. She really liked Jim, had met him on several occasions and understood why Doug trusted him.

Her main concern was Doug, taking on more work. He burned with a passion but candles can burn out, she didn't want him to take on too much. But she would not try to stop him, he was in a love affair and she had no right to interfere.

She felt certain that Jim would suggest seven evenings a week. A total commitment. Doug had mentioned this himself when they had talked backwards and forwards about the next stage. She respected his delight that events were moving forward so rapidly, long neglected needs being met. Oh Doug, my Doug, you are my love. She paused in her thoughts. They never mentioned love, they just got on with things, together. Does the 'L' word need to be defined? Probably not. It hung within and between them, a silent presence in all the hubble and bubble. The unspoken glue that cemented their relationship.

Doug had arranged to attend the songs after that evening's meal and to speak with Jim afterwards.

The hall was packed as usual when they walked in to a warm wave from Jim. He was at the front with his guitar, singing and playing with the group.

They saw Thelma and Wally and walked over to the table they were sharing with another young couple. They were greeted with smiles and waving of arms in time to the music.

Thelma was in fine voice as Tracey pulled up a chair next to her. Doug sat on the other side of the table, next to Wally. He seemed engrossed in the proceedings too, banging Doug happily on the shoulder with an upraised arm. The atmosphere was electric, the whole room singing and waving arms.

As people started to leave, Doug and Tracey said goodbye to Thelma and Wally, and Doug led her into the chapel to wait for Jim. As they sat waiting, Tracey said something Doug did not expect.

'You know Doug, Thelma has a really good voice.'

He looked at her with a questioning expression.

'I mean really good. She probably hasn't had any coaching but boy, that girl can certainly sing.'

Careless words cost lives. In this case they made a life. When Doug got back to the village he called to see choirmaster Gerald, and as the saying goes the rest is history.

Gerald was not often impressed, through the years he had heard many voices and mediocre was the regrettable accolade of his musical profession. His favourite moan was 'surrounded by mediocrity'.

On Doug's recommendation he gave Thelma a trial when the guys next visited Doug, and when she finished the song she had rehearsed there was a pregnant silence. Doug thought she was very good but who was he to express an opinion.

The silence was broken by Gerald's clapping, slowly at first then getting faster and faster, louder and louder, rising on the church acoustics to a vibrating crescendo as he moved towards her from a choir stall.

'My dear, you have a unique talent. Amazing, truly amazing! Your mezzo soprano range is incredible.'

More silence. Wally was lounging in a choir stall on the other side of the aisle, wondering whether he should punch this perv for calling her a messy sopso. The expressions of delight on Doug and Tracey's faces made him push the thought aside. Thelma looked happy, though rather confused.

There was no looking back. Under Gerald's willing tutorship, she started singing beside the trailer, with the small choir at first, then gaining the confidence to sing solo. Always to appreciative applause.

Chapter Thirteen

The latest meeting with Jim had been difficult. A decision had to be made. To stick with the three evenings a week or expand. To four, five? Or go to the whole seven. Doug had the team to manage this, and the need was there. But there could be no going back.

Seven it was. A holy number.

Doug believed if something feels right, no matter what the opposition, go for it. This felt right. Sure there would be problems, a huge commitment which if analysed into its parts would throw up a gigantic No! But the positives far outweighed any negatives.

As he rocked gently in his office chair in the clickie room, Ruby asleep at his feet, he tried to do an analysis of the situation. Vague memories of physics classes emerged. Not his favourite subject at school. Paschen's law is an equation that gives the breakdown voltage, that is, the voltage necessary to start a discharge or electric arc, between two electrodes in a gas as a function of pressure and gap length.

He liked the electric arc idea. There was high voltage at work, a lot of gas sure but a tremendous energy had been generated from a tiny spark.

Harnessing that energy, making it work for future good, channelling it in positive directions, that was his task now.

He sighed heavily. Ruby snored.

Six months passed. Doug grew closer to Thelma and Wally, he collected them from the caravan on several occasions and they stayed with him and Ruby in the cottage. Tracey joined them when she could.

The couple liked the village, and being near to Maidenbury. They enjoyed the peace of the village but also helping Doug with the trailer work. Wally became an accomplished spokesperson for those who required help to challenge authority, putting their case forcefully but with surprising diplomacy.

One day they made a decision, hastened by the council's declaration that the caravan was being permanently removed to the council tip.

With Dawn's help they found a small flat in one of the high rise blocks, and got their almost completed probation orders transferred under Mike Planter's supervision. They obtained good references from their employers in Longmire, and within weeks Mike helped them find similar employment in Maidenbury.

Jim visited a couple of times, offering encouragement and advice. His last visit was a game-changer. Demand was outweighing supply. The trailer van had outlived its usefulness, time to think outside the box. Again.

As Jim walked round Maidenbury with Doug, he pointed to the empty shops.

'There you are, stage two.'

He explained that larger more permanent premises could be rented reasonably. With room for a hall and kitchen facilities. Somewhere warm. No doubt the landlord would agree to any minor interior work to improve the premises, to make them what Doug needed.

Doug got to work, and soon found a large empty shop, central and more or less already what was required. It had been empty for a year and the landlord was more than willing to draw up a lease. The fact that he was a friend of Mike Planter the probation officer helped. Although the idea of the place being filled with the great unwashed every evening did not inspire confidence, a written assurance from Doug to rectify any damage, plus a substantial deposit and the guarantee of a regular monthly income swung the balance.

Two months later Doug and his team had moved in and were serving hot meals to an ever-growing population. Mike Planter sold the trailer back to the original garage of purchase, albeit at a small loss for wear and tear, and Ruby was happy to see the estate parked in the driveway at home again. She had never got used to that hissing thing.

Four months passed, when something extraordinary happened. Doug had been talking with several people, discussing their problems, offering practical help, even to find work. 'The

Happening' as he called it appeared out of nowhere.

The songs were always enjoyed, brought hope and joy to the listeners - after their stomachs were full.

One evening as he was helping to clear away in the shop before the choir started, with Thelma as lead singer, a group at one of the larger tables who had been gesticulating and talking loudly in each other's face, got to their feet.

Oh no, trouble? There was a strict policy about alcohol and drugs, they were not allowed on the premises. However, no matter how vigilant the two team members responsible for keeping an eye out were, on occasion the odd person the worse for wear slipped in. They were not thrown out but fed and watered, under close supervision. And counselled when the culprit had recuperated.

Suddenly this group started shouting, well tried to sing 'He's a jolly good fellow' pointing to Doug, and soon the whole room was on its feet joining in.

Doug was slightly embarrassed, but waved and smiled in appreciation.

That was the moment when a retired nonentity was re-born into the much-loved Rev Doug, non-denominational pastor of a most unusual flock. And part of the shop was transformed into a small chapel.

THE END